The One in the Middle
Is the Green Kangaroo

JUDY BLUME

The One in the Middle
Is the Green Kangaroo

Illustrated by Amy Aitken

A YEARLING BOOK

Published by
Dell Publishing Co., Inc.
1 Dag Hammarskjold Plaza
New York, New York 10017

Text copyright © 1981 by Judy Blume

Illustrations copyright © 1981 by Amy Aitken

Yearling® TM 913705, Dell Publishing Co., Inc.

ISBN 0-440-46731-4

Reprinted by arrangement with The Bradbury Press, Inc.

Printed in the United States of America

Sixth Dell printing—September 1983

CW

For Randy and Larry,
who have been there from the beginning

The One in the Middle
Is the Green Kangaroo

Freddy Dissel had two problems. One was his older brother Mike. The other was his younger sister Ellen. Freddy thought a lot about being the one in the middle. But there was nothing he could do about it. He felt like the peanut butter part of a sandwich, squeezed between Mike and Ellen.

Every year Mike got new clothes. He grew too big for his old ones. But Mike's old clothes weren't too small for Freddy. They fit him just fine.

Freddy used to have a room of his
own. That was before Ellen was born.
Now Ellen had a room of *her* own. Freddy
moved in with Mike. Mom and Dad said,
"It's the boys' room." But they couldn't fool
Freddy. He knew better!

Once Freddy tried to join Mike and his friends. But Mike said, "Get out of the way, kid!" So Freddy tried to play with Ellen. Ellen didn't understand how to play his way. She messed up all of Freddy's things. Freddy got mad and pinched her. Ellen screamed.

"Freddy Dissel!" Mom yelled. "You shouldn't be mean to Ellen. She's smaller than you. She's just a baby!"

Ellen didn't look like a baby to Freddy. She didn't sound like a baby either. She even goes to nursery school, Freddy thought. *Some baby!*

Freddy figured things would never get better for him. He would always be a great big middle nothing!

Then one day Freddy heard about the school play. Mike had never been in a play. Ellen had never been in a play. This was his chance to do something special. Freddy decided he would try it.

He waited two whole days before he went to his teacher. "Ms. Gumber," he said. "I want to be in the school play."

Ms. Gumber smiled and shook her head. "I'm sorry, Freddy," she said. "The play is being done by the fifth and sixth graders. The big boys and girls, like Mike."

Freddy looked at the floor and mumbled. "That figures!" He started to walk away.

"Wait a minute, Freddy," Ms. Gumber called. "I'll talk to Ms. Matson anyway. She's in charge of the play. I'll find out if they need any second graders to help."

Finally, Ms. Gumber told Freddy that Ms. Matson needed someone to play a special part. Ms. Gumber said, "Go to the auditorium this afternoon. Maybe you'll get the part."

"Great!" Freddy hollered.

Later he went to the auditorium. Ms. Matson was waiting for him. Freddy walked right up close to her. He said, "I want to be in the play."

Ms. Matson asked him to go up on the stage and say that again – in a very loud voice.

Freddy had never been on the stage. It was big. It made him feel small. He looked out at Ms. Matson.

"I AM FREDDY," he shouted. "I WANT TO BE IN THE PLAY."

"Good," Ms. Matson called. "Now then Freddy, can you jump?"

What kind of question was that, Freddy wondered. Of course he could jump. He was in second grade, wasn't he? So he jumped. He jumped all around the stage — big jumps and little jumps. When he was through Ms. Matson clapped her hands, and Freddy climbed down from the stage.

"I think you will be fine as the Green Kangaroo, Freddy," Ms. Matson said. "It's a very important part."

Freddy didn't tell anyone at home about the play until dinner time. Then he said, "Guess what, everyone? Guess what I'm going to be?"

No one paid any attention to what Freddy was saying. They were too busy eating.

Dad said, "Freddy, I think it's wonderful that you got the part in the play."

Mom kissed him and said, "We're all proud of you, Freddy."

Ellen laughed. "Green Kangaroo, Green Kangaroo," she said over and over again.

Mike just shook his head and said, "I still can't believe it. *He's* going to be the Green Kangaroo."

"It's true," Freddy said. "Just me. All by myself – the only Green Kangaroo in the play."

The next two weeks were busy ones for Freddy. He had to practice being the Green Kangaroo a lot. He practiced at school on the stage. He practiced at home, too. He made kangaroo faces in front of the mirror. He did kangaroo jumps on his bed. He even dreamed about Green Kangaroos at night.

Finally, the day of the play came. The whole family would be there. Some of their neighbors were coming too.

Mom hugged Freddy extra hard as he left for school. "We'll be there watching you, Green Kangaroo," she said.

After lunch Ms. Gumber called to Freddy. "Time to go now. Time to get into your costume." Ms. Gumber walked to the hall with Freddy.

Then she whispered, "We'll be in the second row. Break a leg."

"Break a leg?" Freddy said.

Ms. Gumber laughed. "That means good luck when you're in a play."

"Oh," Freddy said. "I thought you meant I should fall off the stage and *really* break a leg."

Ms. Gumber laughed again. She ruffled Freddy's hair.

Freddy went to Ms. Matson's room. The girls in the sixth grade had made his costume. They all giggled when Ms. Matson helped Freddy into it. His Green Kangaroo suit covered all of him. It even had green feet. Only his face stuck out. Ms. Matson put some green dots on it. "We'll wash them off later. Okay?"

"Okay," Freddy mumbled. He jumped over to the mirror. He looked at himself. He really felt like a Green Kangaroo.

It was time for the play to begin. Freddy waited backstage with the fifth and sixth graders who were in the play. They looked at him and smiled. He tried to smile back. But the smile wouldn't come. His heart started to beat faster. His stomach bounced up and down. He felt funny. Then Ms. Matson leaned close to him. She said, "They're waiting for you, Freddy. Go ahead."

He jumped out onto the stage. He looked out into the audience. All those people were down there – somewhere. He knew they were. It was very quiet. He could hear his heart. He thought he saw Mom and Dad. He thought he saw Ellen. He thought he saw Mike and Ms. Gumber and his second grade class and all of his neighbors, too. They were all out there somewhere. They were all in the middle of the audience. But Freddy wasn't in the middle. He was all by himself up on the stage. He had a job to do. He *had* to be the Green Kangaroo.

Freddy smiled. His heart slowed down. His stomach stayed still. He felt better. He smiled a bigger, wider smile. He felt good.

"HELLO EVERYONE," Freddy
said. "I AM THE GREEN KAN-
GAROO. WELCOME."

The play began. Freddy did his big
and little jumps. Every few minutes one of
the fifth or sixth graders in the play said to
him, "And who are you?"

Freddy jumped around and
answered. "Me? I am the Green Kangaroo!" It was easy. That was all he had to
say. It was fun, too. Every time he said it
the audience laughed. Freddy liked it
when they laughed. It was a funny play.

When it was all over everyone on the
stage took a bow. Then Ms. Matson came
out and waited for the audience to get
quiet. She said, "A special thank you to our
second grader, Freddy Dissel. He played
the part of the Green Kangaroo."

Freddy jumped over to the middle of the stage. He took a big, low bow all by himself. The audience clapped hard for a long time.

Freddy didn't care much about wearing Mike's clothes any more. He didn't care much about sharing Mike's room either. He didn't care much that Ellen was small and cute. He didn't even care much about being the one in the middle. He felt just great being Freddy Dissel.

Have hours of fun playing paper dolls!

Beverly Cleary
Cutting Up with Ramona

It features the irresistible Ramona Quimby, big sister Beezus, their pal Henry Huggins, and his fearless dog Ribsy. Illustrations in full color by JoAnn Scribner. 9″ x 12″ $3.50

Nate the Great

noses out seven tricky mysteries.

Written by Marjorie Weinman Sharmat

Neighborhood detective Nate and his faithful dog Sludge are among young readers' favorite sleuths. Read their deliciously funny adventures in:

_____ NATE THE GREAT $1.50 (46126-X)
_____ NATE THE GREAT AND THE LOST LIST $1.25 (46282-7)
_____ NATE THE GREAT AND THE MISSING KEY ...$1.95 (46191-X)
_____ NATE THE GREAT AND THE PHONY CLUE....$1.25 (46300-9)
_____ NATE THE GREAT AND THE STICKY CASE....$1.25 (46289-4)
_____ NATE THE GREAT GOES UNDERCOVER $1.50 (46302-5)
_____ NATE THE GREAT AND THE SNOWY TRAIL...$1.95 (46276-2)

YEARLING BOOKS

At your local bookstore or use this handy coupon for ordering:

 DELL BOOKS
P.O. BOX 1000, PINE BROOK, N.J. 07058-1000

Please send me the books I have checked above. I am enclosing $ _____ (please add 75c per copy to cover postage and handling). Send check or money order—no cash or C.O.D.'s. Please allow up to 8 weeks for shipment.

Name _____

Address _____

City _____ State/Zip _____